Gabriella's Song

BY
Candace Fleming
❦

ILLUSTRATED BY
Giselle Potter
❦

AN ANNE SCHWARTZ BOOK

ATHENEUM BOOKS FOR YOUNG READERS

For Anne Schwartz, whose thoughtful comments and
insightful suggestions truly made Gabriella sing
—C. F.

To Mom, Chloe, and Dad
—G. P.

The artwork for this book consists of ink, watercolors, and colored pencils.

Atheneum Books for Young Readers
An imprint of Simon & Schuster Children's Publishing Division
1230 Avenue of the Americas
New York, New York 10020
Text copyright © 1997 by Candace Fleming
Illustrations copyright © 1997 by Giselle Potter
Book design by Angela Carlino
The text of this book is set in Mrs. Eaves.
First Edition
Printed in Hong Kong by South China
Printing Co. (1988) Ltd.
10 9 8 7 6 5 4 3 2 1

Library of Congress Cataloging-in-Publication Data
Fleming, Candace.
Gabriella's song / by Candace Fleming ; illustrated
by Giselle Potter.—1st ed.
p. cm.
"An Anne Schwartz book."
Summary: A young girl finds music all around her
as she walks about the city of Venice, Italy, and she shares
her song with everyone she meets.
ISBN 0-689-80973-5
[1. Music—Fiction. 2. Venice (Italy)—Fiction.]
I. Potter, Giselle, ill. II. Title.
PZ7.F59936Gaf 1997
[E]—DC20   96-2459

Author's Note

Once upon a time, Venice was truly the city of music. Concertos, contatas, and arias could be heard almost everywhere—in churches and palaces, public squares and private homes, ballrooms and classrooms, even in the streets. No other European city could match Venice's passion for music.

Opera was born here. From the moment it was introduced in 1607, Venetians embraced this new art form, building themselves the first opera house in Europe, then flocking to its performances. And what performances they were! Opera made audiences laugh. It made them cry. It made them shout, or cheer, or gasp with fear. It was the perfect combination of story and song, and Venetians couldn't get enough of it.

Even today in Venice you can hear arias in the opera houses. You can hear contatas in the churches and the songs of street performers in the piazzas. And, if you listen very closely, you just might hear a little girl humming as she skips through the narrow, winding streets.

Ah, Venice! The city of the Piazza San Marco. The Grand Canal.
St. Mark's Cathedral.

But to Gabriella Menza, Venice was something more. Venice was the city of music.

On her way home from the marketplace, Gabriella heard the
morning melody of the street traders singing their wares:
"Fresh, fresh fish!"
"Hot pie, hot!"
"Buy my sweet, sweet cream!"
She heard the rhythm of the tethered boats thumping against the
canal walls. *Bump de bump bump. Bump de bump bump.*

And echoing in harmony down the paved alleyways and between the high buildings, she heard the *slap-slap* of drying laundry; the *flap-flap* of pigeon wings; the *jing-aling-ling* of lire; and the *ting-aling-ling* of church bells.

Then, way in the distance rising sweet and clear, Gabriella heard her mother's call.

"Gabriella! Gabriella *amore mio*! Come home!"

Her mother's voice mingled with the city's sounds. And within Gabriella's heart they blended and blurred and became a song.

Humming the song that sprang to her lips, Gabriella skipped down the lane toward home.

As she passed Pagliani's Bakery, she decided to stop for a
morning pastry.

"One cannoli please, Signor Pagliani," Gabriella told the baker.
While she waited she hummed her song.

"What is that you're singing?" asked Pagliani.

"Just a little tune," replied Gabriella. She hummed louder so he
could hear.

The baker whistled a few bars himself. "Why, that's good," he
declared. "It makes my heart light and my feet feel like dancing."

"I like it too," agreed Gabriella. She handed Pagliani a coin,
took her cannoli, and, still humming, skipped out the door.

Gabriella's song stayed behind. The baker whistled it while kneading dough. He whistled it while filling pastries. He whistled it while waiting on the widow Santucci.

"Ah," sighed the widow. "Such a sad song. It makes me long for my younger, happier days."

"Really?" replied Pagliani. "It makes me feel younger and happier."

The widow blew her nose. "Songs mean different things to different people. If it makes you happy, then whistle away, Signor. Whistle away."

Picking up her shopping basket, the widow Santucci left the bakery with four loaves of bread and Gabriella's song.

As she climbed into a gondola, the widow began to hum.

"That's a catchy tune!" cried Luigi the gondolier. "What is it?"

"I do not know," replied the widow. "I heard it from the baker. It's so sad, no?"

"No!" exclaimed the gondolier. "That's not a sad song. That's a love song. Listen."

He clutched his accordion to his heart and played Gabriella's song.

Now the music wafted and weaved on the breeze.
It alighted on the ears of the other gondoliers gliding
through the waterways who snatched up their accordions
and joined in.

It wound its way down the streets, where housewives heard it
and hummed.
Dockworkers listened, then whistled.
Schoolchildren sang aloud.
Gabriella's song reverberated throughout all of Venice.

But one man did not hear it—the brilliant composer Giuseppe Del Pietro. Instead, he sat at his piano staring at the black-and-white keys.

In just a few weeks, the composer was expected to perform his newest symphony in the Piazza San Marco. But after months of hard work, he still could not create the simplest tune. For the first time in his career, Giuseppe Del Pietro could not find the music.

Frustrated, Giuseppe pushed away from his piano and walked to the window. He opened it wide.

Like a miracle, the music found him. Rising to greet him from below came the sweetest tune he had ever heard.

The composer leaned out his window and looked down. There, at the doorway of his very own building, Gabriella's mother was saying, "Sing it again, *mio amore*. I want to remember it always."

So Gabriella sang.

Her mother smiled. She swayed, eyes shut tight.

Above them, Giuseppe shut his eyes too and gave himself up to the music. In the notes he heard the *slap-slap* of drying laundry and the *flap-flap* of pigeon wings. He heard the *jing-aling-ling* of *lire* and the *ting-aling-ling* of church bells. And above it all, he heard the clear, sweet call of *"Mio amore! Mio amore!"*

"That's it!" Giuseppe cried. Snatching the song from the air, he dashed to his piano and scribbled furiously in his notebook. Then he played back what he had written.

"Bellissima!" he exclaimed. "But it is not finished. It needs more."

Day and night the composer worked. He added an opening movement, a scherzo, and a grand finale. He turned Gabriella's song into a symphony.

Weeks later, music lovers from all over Venice filled the Piazza
San Marco to hear Del Pietro's newest work.
Luigi and his fellow gondoliers were there.

So were the widow Santucci and Pagliani the baker.
And Gabriella, sitting beside her mother, was there.

A hush fell over the audience as the composer raised his baton. He gave the downbeat. Instantly, the orchestra burst into life.

The music soared and swirled. It climbed. It curled. It grew higher and higher and higher still, until strings, woodwinds, and percussion met in a heart-stopping crescendo.

The audience shivered from the music's beauty. In the familiar tune they heard laundry and pigeons, *lire* and church bells. They heard happiness and sadness and love. The audience knew that this was, by far, Del Pietro's greatest symphony.

The music faded.
The audience sprang to its feet.
"*Bravo!*" they applauded. "*Bravissimo!*"
Giuseppe Del Pietro turned to face the admiring crowd. "*Grazie*,"
he said, bowing. "But I alone cannot take credit for this music. Weeks
ago I was inspired by a simple song I heard outside my window. To
whoever was singing, I now say *grazie*."

In the audience, the gondoliers turned toward Luigi.
Luigi turned toward the widow Santucci.
The widow turned toward Pagliani the baker.
The baker turned toward Gabriella.

And Gabriella turned toward her mother. Wide smiles spread across both their faces.

"Take a bow, *mio amore*," her mother urged. "Take a bow."